Bigfoot
and
Lightning Bug

Written & Illustrated by
Donell Barlow

Bigfoot and Lightning Bug

© 2019 by Donell Barlow. All rights reserved.

Printed in the United States.
ISBN: 978-0-578-54972-9

DonellBarlow.com

Dedicated to Grandma Vera
and my daughter, Dusk.

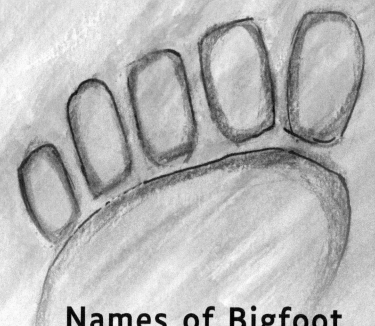

Names of Bigfoot

Sc'weney'ti (Giant, Bigfoot)
Salish language, spoken by Spokane Tribe

Wo-nue raa-yor' (Ridgerunner)
Yurok language, spoken by Yurok Tribe

Saabe (Bigfoot)
Anishinaabemowin, spoken by Ojibwe Tribes

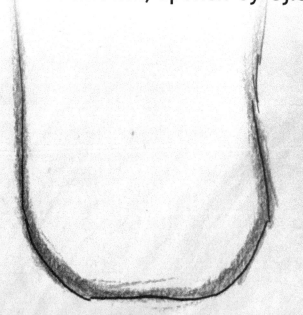

Hello, new friend. My name is Lightning Bug. I would like to share a story with you, because I need your help to protect our forests and animals.

It begins with my Grandma.
She told me the best stories, and my favorite stories were about Bigfoot.

"Any encounter with a Bigfoot is special," Grandma told me. "They are connected to our Mother Earth. You will know when one is close by, Lightning Bug. Their smell is strong and hard to miss."

I knew the forest would be the best place to meet my new friend.

Fingers crossed, on the way to the mountain today I will get my wish.

Pit-pat, pit-pat,
walking through the forest.

Peee-yewww.

Something smells stinky. Could it be my new best friend?

"Holy smoke signals, it's a Bigfoot!"

"Hello, my name is Benny. Can we be best friends?' he said.

"Of course!" I said. "Follow me, bestie."

Benny and I made it to the sweet
spot on the mountain.

We found heaps of huckleberries
that turned our tongues purple.

Riding piggyback all the way home, I held onto Benny's thick, scraggly fur.

I wonder what else hitched a
ride in his fur today.

Momma was thrilled to meet Benny, and
she greeted him with a warm hug.

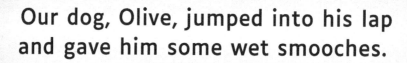

Our dog, Olive, jumped into his lap
and gave him some wet smooches.

Lick, lick, lick.

Momma said, "Please get cleaned up for dinner, and take Benny with you."

Chhh, chhh, chhh.

Momma cooked us up a pile of butter
noodles for dinner.

Benny and I had huge appetites.

Slurp, slurp, slurp.

"Time for bed," said Momma.

Benny snored so loud it shook the house,
and Olive and I had to cover our ears.

Z Zzzz,

ZZZZ,

ZZZZ.

It's morning! Time to go out and play.
Momma and Olive came with us, too.

A game of hide and seek—against Benny,
who is the current champion.

Clap, clap, clap.

Down by the river, we found a lot of garbage.
Momma looked sad.

"We must clean this trash up right away, and put it where it belongs," Momma said.

Benny came down to help us.

"Now that I have seen your world,
I invite you to come see mine.
Follow me," Benny said.

"This is a magical doorway that leads to the
secret gathering place for the animal council."

"I want to help, and I pledge to protect the forest."

"I knew I could count on you, Lightning Bug," Benny said.

"I must go now. We will see each other soon."

Momma kissed me on the cheek.
"I'm so proud of you, Lightning Bug," she said.
"You can do anything you set your mind to. It's
time for us to go home now, too."

Donations for the Forest

A portion of the proceeds from the sale of this book is donated to The Lands Council, which supports the protection of the forests, waters, and wildlife of the Inland Northwest.

Thank you for pledging to do your part to protect the forest and take care of the animals!

The Lands Council
25 W. Main, Suite 222, Spokane, WA
<u>landscouncil.org</u>

About the Author

Donell Barlow is a storyteller, activist, holistic health coach, yoga teacher, and hairdresser. She was raised in Spokane, Washington, by her single father and still lives in the Pacific Northwest. Donell's Native American heritage is Yurok and Ottawa. Her daughter, Dusk, was born in 2018.

Connect with Donell at <u>DonellBarlow.com</u>.

Photograph by Robert I. Mesa Photography

About the Book Design

Reading can be hard for Bigfoots, and sometimes it's hard for people, too. So the text of *Bigfoot and Lightning Bug* is set in Luciole, a font designed to provide the best reading experience for people with dyslexia and other reading or visual processing disabilities. Luciole is French for "firefly." Learn more at luciole-vision.com/luciole-en.html.

Digital layout and art editing by Anna Morgan.
Book design by Accessibility First.
ThinkAccessibilityFirst.com

CPSIA information can be obtained
at www.ICGtesting.com
Printed in the USA
LVHW071251290122
709691LV00002B/3